JOHNNY TALL DOG

Leo P. Kelley

LEARNING · DEVELOPMENT · AIDS

Johnny Tall Dog
LD875S
ISBN 1 85503 013 6
© Fearon Education
Published under licence in the UK by LDA
All rights reserved
First published in UK 1990

LDA, Duke Street, Wisbech, Cambs., PE13 2AE England

Printed in Great Britain by Ebenezer Baylis and Son Ltd,
The Trinity Press, Worcester, and London.

1

Belonging

I rode toward the north, the morning sun burning in the sky off my right shoulder. The sweat slid down my back in a river. My horse, too was wet from the morning's hard ride over the prairie.

But the prairie grass all around us was dry. It popped and cracked like small fires as we made our way through it.

On a distant rise, the trees looked like thirsty people with their arms lifted to the sky. I wondered if anyone watched me from that rise. What must I have looked like?

Once I heard a man I had beaten in a fair fight say these words about me: "He's like a tree — tall, wide at the top and narrow further down. And like a tree, he holds his ground."

Often I have heard these words whispered by people who don't trust me: "His hair is too black and straight. And look! It hangs too far down his back."

My eyes are dark, almost black. I notice this when I catch them looking back at me from a pool of water. And my skin is dark — very near the colour of the clay soil that lays beyond the prairie.

I had told myself I belonged with that red soil. I belonged with the prairie I saw all around me. I was riding home.

A north wind began to blow. It beat the tall prairie grass and made the land itself seem as if it was moving. Then something *was* moving. Two men were riding towards me from the west. They were riding hard, ropes in hand, chasing down two oxen.

I watched for a moment, then quickly turned my horse and rode toward the oxen to head them off. Just before I reached them, the oxen broke to the right and turned back the way they had come.

As the cattle ran back, the two riders threw their ropes neatly, catching the oxen around their necks. The ropes held tight and brought the cattle to a stop.

When the dust had settled, one of the riders tipped his hat to me.

"Thanks," he said. "Thanks for the help, Mr . . ."

"Johnny," I said and tipped my black hat back to him.

The man gave out a big laugh. "Well, *Johnny*," he said, "I do thank you. If you hadn't come along we'd probably still be chasing those oxen."

"All the way to St. Louis," his partner added. He smiled through his thick, grey beard.

"Just glad to help," I said.

"You riding out here all alone?" the man with the laugh wanted to know.

I told him I was, and he shook his head. "The Sioux sometimes ride this far south looking for buffalo," he told me. "You should keep your eyes open. If they see you first, you're as good as dead."

"No good Indians!" the man with the beard said. "The day can't come soon enough when every last one of them's been killed!"

I looked at the anger in his blue eyes and at the fear in his partner's brown eyes.

"I can look after myself." I said.

"Well, I hope you can handle that gun you're carrying," the man with the beard said.

I put my hand on the Colt .45 and smiled back at him. "Never been a problem."

"Well, then," said the man with the laugh. "We wish you luck. We'd best be heading back to the herd. Thanks again for your help."

I sat still in the saddle as I watched the two men ride off across the prairie. The words of the bearded man rang in my mind. *The day can't come soon enough when every last one of them's been killed!*

I wondered what they would have done if they had known I was part Indian. Or that my father was a full-blooded Sioux.

I remembered the angry look in the blue eyes and reached down to touch my Colt .45.

*   *   *

It was two days later on the Oregon Trail when I spotted the covered wagon. It was just sitting there in the middle of the trail. A team of oxen was hitched up in front, and a horse was tied on behind.

It was strange to come across a single wagon that way. Wagons didn't often travel the trail alone. If something went wrong, there was no one around to help. This might have been a wagon left behind by a wagon train — except for the animals. Unless the animals were sick, they never would have been left behind.

I was moving closer when my horse snorted and tossed his head high in the air. He tried to run, but I brought him to a stop.

My eyes searched the ground in front of me. There was no sign of snakes or anything else that would have set the horse off. Could it have been the wagon? I listened carefully but could hear no sounds coming from it.

Suddenly my horse tried to run again. This time I looked back over my shoulder and saw what the trouble was. Off in the east, a prairie fire ran in a long red line, cutting straight across the trail. It was coming my way. Its tall flames seemed to touch the sky. They danced and leaped as they ate the grass that lay before them.

I would have to ride and ride hard if I hoped to keep ahead of the racing fire. With luck I could keep in front of it until it burned itself out. Then I remembered the wagon.

"Hello in the wagon!" I called out.

No one answered.

Hello!" I called again, louder.

At last a face appeared in the opening at the back. It was a young woman. But as she began to answer, she saw the prairie fire behind me. Her eyes fixed on it, and she couldn't move.

"You've got to leave your wagon here," I told her. "Get on your horse. There's no time to lose. Prairie fires travel as fast as trains. Is anyone in the wagon with you?"

"My husband Charles."

"Get him quick. Both of you get on your horse. There's no time to waste. You've got to keep ahead of the fire."

"But we can't ride!" she said. "I mean, Charles can't. He's too sick."

A picture formed in my mind. If the couple couldn't ride away, they would be caught in the fire for sure. There was only one thing to try. It might save us all — or get us all killed.

Quickly I got down from my horse and tied him to the back of the wagon. "Put something over the horses' eyes!" I ordered.

The woman did as she was told. She reached behind her and picked up some pieces of cloth. Then she jumped down from the wagon and tied them around the horses' heads.

That was good to do, I thought. If the horses couldn't see the fire, they would be less afraid when the flames came near.

I took two shirts and some matches from my saddle-bag and ran to the front of the wagon. I tied the shirts over the oxen's eyes. Then I went a short way from the big animals and lit a match. The wind blew it out. It blew out the next match too. The same wind was blowing the prairie fire closer and closer.

Quickly I ran to my horse to get my bedroll. I hurried back with it to the front of the wagon. The wind was blowing hard to the west as I pulled the blanket over my head and shoulders. But under the blanket, with the wind at my back, I was at last able to keep a match lit. I touched it to the ground in front of me. The dry grass quickly caught fire. As the wind blew from the east, the new fire spread to the west, away from the wagon.

Just then the woman came running around the side of the oxen. She was looking at me as if I was crazy. "What are you doing?" she yelled. "Now we've got fire in front of us as well as behind!"

I just shouted at her to get up on the wagon. Then I took the collar of one of the oxen and slapped the big animal on the rear. With a hard pull, I started both of the oxen moving forward slowly. I kept them following the path of the fire I had set. Soon they stood with the wagon in the middle of the black space where all the prairie grass had been burned away.

"Now hold the oxen by the rings!" I told the woman. "And don't let them move!"

The woman hooked her fingers into the rings that went through the oxen's noses. I ran around the wagon to where the horses were stamping nervously. I talked to them and held their reins tightly as the prairie fire moved closer. Soon the heat became so bad that sweat poured from my body. I had to turn my face toward the wagon.

In seconds I heard the loud noise of the fire

rushing past us. Without grass to burn, it left the wagon untouched.

But suddenly the horses and I were being pulled forward. The wagon was moving!

"Stop those oxen!" I shouted to the woman.

"Hold them back!"

But the wagon kept moving. It turned wildly to the left, then to the right. As it did, the frightened horses tried to break free, but I was able to hold onto them. Suddenly shots rang out, and the wagon came to a stop.

I removed the cloths that covered the horses' eyes and rushed around to the front of the wagon. There I found the woman sitting quietly on the driver's seat, a blank look on her face. In her hand was a gun. She didn't move. She sat looking down at the oxen that lay dead on the ground in front of her.

"The fool beasts got scared," she said. "I had to shoot them. I couldn't hold them, and they were heading right into the fire."

She looked past me with her blank grey eyes. "Charles and I never did belong here," she said. "And now we'll never make it to Oregon. Without animals to pull the wagon, we're done for."

2

Death Rides the Trail

"You're not done for," I told the woman. "You're still alive, aren't you?"

"I guess you're right," the woman said. Then she shook her head. "It just can't be too much longer before Charles will be well," she told herself. Then she turned and pushed back the cloth that covered the opening to the wagon. "Charles?" she called in a soft voice. "Charles? How do you feel?"

There was no answer.

"Charles?" she called again. She stood up and climbed into the back of the wagon. She spoke his name once more, then made a long, low moan.

I jumped onto the driver's seat and looked inside the opening. The woman was bending over her husband, who lay on a bed on the floor of the wagon.

"He's dead," she said when she saw me. She stared at me as if she couldn't believe it. "Dead," she said again.

I moved into the wagon and pressed a finger against the side of the man's neck. No pulse there. The skin was cold. "I'm sorry," I told the woman, but she just turned away.

I moved back to the driver's seat, where I sat for a few minutes looking out over the prairie. In front of me lay the dead oxen. Behind me in the wagon lay the woman's dead husband. All around me the land had been turned black by fire. Death seemed to be everywhere. It was a hard land, this country I was coming back to. You had to fight it with everything you had if you wanted to stay alive.

In a while, the woman appeared beside me on the driver's seat. Her eyes were dry, but her mouth was stretched in a tight line. She seemed to want to say something, but no words would come to her.

At last I asked, "Do you have a shovel?"

"A shovel?" She looked puzzled. Then she understood. "Yes, " she said. "I have one."

The sun crossed the top of the sky and started down in the west as I dug. For a while the woman watched, without talking, from the driver's seat. Then she went inside the wagon. She was still there when I looked in the wagon to tell her I had finished digging.

"He's ready," she said. "He's wearing his best shirt."

I tried to smile. "He looks fine," I told her.

Then together the two of us lifted the body out of the wagon and placed it in the ground. As she looked down at the man, the lines around her eyes wrinkled. She looked far older then her years.

"I should say something," the woman said. "But I don't know what."

"Say what is in your heart."

Her eyes met mine, then looked down and closed. In a moment, the words came. They were simple but true. "Charles, I'll miss you. I wish you could have lived to see the better times we hoped for."

She turned her face away then, and I figured she was crying. I pushed the shovel quietly into the earth to begin the job of filling the grave.

But she turned quickly and caught my wrist with a strong grip of her hand. Her dry eyes stared up into my face, and I understood. I let go of the shovel, and she filled the grave herself.

While she worked, I went over to my horse. I took some sticks from a bundle I found inside the wagon. Then I made a small fire and made some coffee.

The woman came to join me by the fire and drank some coffee. After a while, she spoke. "I haven't thanked you yet for saving my life. My name is Nan Powers. And I do thank you." She held out her hand.

"I'd have done the same for anyone in trouble," I told her. "My name is Johnny. And I'm glad you're alive." I shook her hand and felt its firm grip again. Then I sat back from the fire and looked at where the sun was in the sky. "Will you be going on to Oregon?" I asked.

"I don't know," she said. "The wagon train we started out with is far ahead of us now. We had planned to catch up with it at Fort Early once Charles got better. But it's been days since we've been on the trail. Now that

Charles is dead, I should get going fast, I guess."

I agreed with Nan. She stirred the fire with a stick. Then she looked up at me.

"Where are you heading, Johnny?"

"North," I said.

My answer caught her by surprise. "What on earth for? That's Indian country. The Sioux will lift your hair if you go up there."

"I've been there before," I told Nan. "No Indian took my scalp then. I think I can keep my scalp this time too."

"I've heard that Sitting Bull has run off from the reservation with some of his braves," Nan went on. "He's camped somewhere in the direction you're heading."

"I've heard that too."

"I've also heard that Custer took a group of soldiers into the Black Hills in 1874 — just last year. They found gold up there."

I nodded. I remembered the stories I had heard about the gold and about Custer. When I looked back at Nan, she was pointing a finger straight at me.

"Gold!" she cried, proud to have found the answer. *"That's* why you're going north. I don't blame you though, Johnny. I wouldn't mind finding gold myself. I've never been anything in my life but poor."

"The Black Hills are part of the Sioux reservation," I told her. "The government let the Sioux have the land when they promised not to make war again. No one but the Indians are allowed on the reservation without special permission from the government."

Nan shrugged. "Well, sometimes the government looks the other way. They don't care all that much about Indians. You must know that."

I studied the grey eyes but found no anger there. "I know," I said. "But that doesn't make it right."

"No, it doesn't." Nan shook her head. "Well, mining for gold probably isn't for me anyway. I'm not the lucky kind. I guess I'll just make my way west. That's what I'll do — keep going west, all the way to Oregon."

As Nan spoke, I saw a very young woman behind the lines in the hard face. I felt I might be able to help her once again.

"You can ride along with me if you want some company," I found myself saying. "Then when we get close to Indian land, you can head on west."

"Don't get any fancy ideas!" Nan snapped suddenly. "You came along at the right time, and I thank you for that. But you can keep your own company. I can make it from here on my own!"

"I think you've got the wrong idea, Nan. But think it over. You suit yourself."

I poured the rest of the coffee over the fire. Then I went to the back of the wagon and untied my horse. I was about to step up into the saddle when Nan came over to me. A six-gun was strapped to her waist.

"You're probably going to run into some Sioux where you're headed, Johnny," she said.

"I might."

"Well, now that I think about it, the two of us riding together would have a better chance against them than one man riding alone."

I looked down at the young woman and at the determined look on her face. I nodded. "I do believe you're right, Nan."

"I'll get my rifle and a few other things. But what should I do with the wagon?"

"Not much to do but leave it here," I explained. "Some other family heading west can probably use the wagon and the things in it."

Nan came back with her rifle and the few belongings she would tie to her saddle. She saddled her horse, and mounted up to leave. As we started down the trail, Nan turned to take one last look at the pile of rocks that marked her husband's grave.

She was still for a moment, her eyes fixed on the spot. Then she gave her horse a hard kick and went flying on ahead of me. I had to ride hard to catch up with her. She seemed to be trying to get as far away from the place as fast as she could.

* * *

Time on the prairie passed slowly. Each day's ride was a long one, from sunrise to sunset. As we travelled north across Nebraska, we got closer to the Black Hills of South Dakota.

The colour of the sky changed from blue to grey as we neared the end of the third day's ride. When we crossed the last rise that day, we saw a farm. A small stone house and a barn were built on the prairie below us. The farm was at the edge of a row of trees by a river. The fields were green. A warm yellow glow came from one small window of the house. A trail of white smoke curled out of its chimney.

"Looks like we're in luck today, Johnny," Nan said. "Might get a warm place to sleep and a home-cooked meal."

I smiled at the idea — not for long. That was when the gunshot rang out, and the bullet went whistling over our heads.

CHAPTER

3

Hard Words

"Get down off your horses!" a woman's voice shouted at us. "And keep your hands up high where I can see them!"

Then I saw the woman in the darkness. She was standing by the barn with a rifle pointed straight at us. A dog was at her side.

Then the dog turned to look back. A man was standing in the doorway of the house.

"Louise Collins!" the man cried. "What do you think you're doing, woman? We already got enough meat for the table." He laughed. "Put down that rifle and ask these folks what their business is."

"Now, Ed, you know we can't be too sure of strangers."

19

The big man laughed again. He stared at Nan and me. "They aren't Indians," he said.

"So I expect they're OK. Let them come in."

He took the rifle from the woman. It looked like a stick in his large hands.

"We're just passing through," I explained. "We thought we might bed down in your barn for the night."

Collins just nodded. "Sure," he said. "Why not? Won't trouble the cows."

Mrs. Collins smiled then. "It will be nice to have company," she said. "Come on in. We're about to eat."

As all of us ate, the talk went on and on. Life on the prairie farm was lonely, and Ed and Louise Collins were glad to meet other people. They wanted to find out all about us.

"Where are you from, Johnny?" Mrs. Collins asked me.

"Back east," I explained, and she asked if I had a family there. "No," I said. "My mother died there a month ago."

"Oh, I'm sorry about that," Mrs. Collins said. "Is your father living?"

"Yes."

I waited for the next question, but it didn't come. Instead Mrs. Collins turned to Nan. When Nan told about the prairie fire and the death of her husband, Mrs. Collins reached out and touched her hand.

Collins himself just watched, his jaw moving steadily up and down as he ate. Then he turned to me and asked me where the two of us were heading.

"Nan's heading for Oregon," I answered. "And I'm heading north."

"You mean the Black Hills, don't you?" Collins asked. His blue eyes lit up. "Going to look for gold up there, aren't you?"

I just shook my head no. Then I bent my head to take another mouthful of food.

"Well, what is it then?" Collins said. "There's nothing up there but gold and Sioux."

"I have my reasons."

Collins shook his head. "Must be gold." He took a shiny gold watch out of his pocket and set it down on the table. He looked at it proudly for a moment. Then he stuffed a big bite into his mouth and talked around the food. "I'd like to go up to hunt for gold myself. But Louise doesn't take kindly to the idea."

"The Black Hills are part of the Sioux reservation," Mrs. Collins said without looking up from her plate. "The land belongs to the Sioux."

Collins laughed. "The government let Custer and some people go up there last year, didn't they? Why not a few more?"

Mrs. Collins looked at her husband and then away.

"Indians!" Collins spat the word out. "You can't trust a single one of them. They'd kill you as quick as look at you. Why, look at what the Sioux did to those soldiers near Fort Kearney back in '66. Killed every one of them, they did!"

"The Sioux have lived in peace since then," I broke in. "And they killed then because their land was being taken. The same way the whites are trying to take their last piece of land now, bit by bit."

Collins gave me a hard look. He pulled at his beard. "It sounds to me like you're standing up for the Indians."

I was just telling the story the way I know it."

That was when Nan put her hand on mine and broke into the talk. "This has been a wonderful meal, Mrs. Collins. I can't tell you what a joy it is to have had some home cooking!"

After that, we talked about raising food and animals on the prairie. The Collinses told how their supplies had to come all the way from Fort Early. And how they had to dig in for the winter. As they spoke, I remembered the bitter winters of my childhood. Finally I found my hat, said good-night, and walked out to the barn.

A still-warm darkness had fallen outside. An owl's wings beat the air softly. Small animals made noises in the brush. Against these gentle sounds, the words of Ed Collins came back to my ears. *Gold. Black Hills. Indians.* Mix those words together, and you were sure to have trouble. The hunger for gold would bring pain and death to the land and the people. In time, blood would mix with dust.

*   *   *

After a good breakfast, Nan and I set off early the next morning. A gentle wind was blowing, and it took a while for the day to get hot. We rode along quietly. We had talked a long time in the barn the night before. Now we were lost in our own thoughts.

After a time, we saw some riders on a rise ahead of us. They stopped and watched us for a few minutes as we came up the trail toward them. Then suddenly they turned their horses and came riding our way. It didn't take long to figure out who they were.

"Indians!" Nan yelled.

She grabbed for her rifle. But before she could even raise it, I knocked it out of her hands.

4

The Sioux Camp

"Don't shoot," I told Nan.

She looked at me as though I had lost my mind. She started to reach for her six-gun, but I stopped her from drawing.

"Leave it where it is," I said.

Her eyes flashed white — partly in anger, partly in fear.

"Trust me," I said.

By then the Sioux were upon us. There were seven braves in all. They didn't look friendly, but none of them were wearing war paint. They formed a circle around us on their horses. Some of them looked straight at our faces, studying our eyes.

After a minute, one of them spoke. "You

come here to hunt the buffalo?" he asked in English.

I just made a sign for no. But Nan couldn't hold her tongue. "We were just passing through, that's all," she said nervously. "No hunting. And now we'll just be on our way, if that's all right with you."

She started to move her horse forward. But the circle of Sioux closed more tightly around us.

"Why do you come here?" asked the brave who had spoken before.

This time I answered. I told them that we did not come to hunt for buffalo or for gold. And I spoke in the Sioux language.

The brave's face showed great surprise. *"How is it that you know our language?"* he asked me, putting his question this time in the Sioux tongue.

Still speaking Sioux, I answered. *"I grew up with the Sioux,"* I explained. *"My name is Tall Dog."*

What are you saying to them?" Nan wanted to know. I could feel her eyes on me. "How come you can talk their language, Johnny?"

The brave paid no attention to Nan or her words. My Sioux words and the name of Tall

Dog had changed the way he looked at me.

"There was a Tall Dog," he went on. "But Tall Dog went long ago to the land where the sun rises."

"He did," I agreed, "Now he has come back to the land of his father."

"He lies," one of the other braves broke in suddenly. "Tall Dog was a fighter. This one rides with a woman. And he did not try to fight us when we rode down upon him."

I stared the brave down with my eyes and made the sign for no. "Woman?" I said. "This woman would have killed you if I had not stopped her. Tall Dog fights," I explained. "But Tall Dog does not kill his own people."

"You say you are Tall Dog," said the brave who had spoken first. "How do we know if you are telling the truth?"

"My mother was captured in an attack on a wagon train. She was taken to the Sioux camp. There she came to be loved by the Chief Running Bear. He took her to be his wife. A son was born to them. Chief Running Bear named the boy Tall Dog."

"Johnny!" Nan whispered. "What kind of

stupid thing are you up to? Let me in on it."

The braves looked at one another as Nan tried to get my ear. I wanted to explain to Nan, but there wasn't time. I could tell by the way the braves looked that they were beginning to believe my story. I waved Nan quiet.

"Years passed," I went on. "My mother longed to see again the land where the sun rises. She knew that one day the Sioux and the white people would have to learn to live together. And she wanted her son, Tall Dog, to learn about the world from the white people's schools. But Chief Running Bear did not want her to go."

As I spoke, I remembered a night many years ago as if no time has passed at all. In the tepees of the Sioux camp, all were asleep. I awoke to the feel of a hand across my mouth. My mother's face was above me in the tepee. Her blue eyes told me I must be quiet.

Outside the tepee, there were no sounds except for the night call of an owl and the gentle sound of the horses. The smell of burned wood hung in the air, although the fires were long since dead.

To my young boy's eyes, the camp had a magic to it. It was a magic I couldn't quite believe I was leaving. But I took my mother's hand and followed her as she took me to the horses. We led them slowly out of the sleeping camp. At the fall of each heavy hoof, I expected to see someone looking out from a tepee. But no one woke. And soon the camp was far behind us.

We rode all night down a stream that twisted across the wild land. By morning we were far away. In days . . .

I blinked the picture away and looked at the braves as I finished my story. I told them how I had come to the white people's cities.

"I have lived since then with the white people," I said to the braves. *"I come now to see Chief Running Bear and to speak with him. I bring him news of the woman who was his."*

The brave who had spoken first rode up next to me. He put out a strong hand and let it rest on my shoulder. *"You are welcome, Tall Dog. It is good you have come home again. Do you come to stay?"*

"I don't know."

The brave turned to Nan. Still speaking in Sioux, he asked me about her. *"Is this woman yours? Is that why she rides with you?"*

I looked then at Nan, who sat angrily on her horse.

"My friend has met with trouble on the trail," I answered in English. "But she is brave and strong. Her travels will take her to the land where the sun sets."

With a last look at the woman who rode beside me, the brave nodded. Then he spoke a few more words of Sioux and turned his pony. He and the six other braves began riding north.

"What did you say to them?" Nan asked. "It must have been really good to get them to ride off like that and let us be."

I put my hand out to Nan. "It's time for us to part ways." I told her. "Head towards where the sun sets. Follow the trail to the west, through the mountains. It will take you to Oregon."

Nan didn't take my hand. She didn't even notice that I had put it out to shake hands with her. She was studying my face.

"I must ride with the Sioux braves," I said.

"Why?" she wanted to know. "Did you make some kind of deal with them to save my skin?"

"No," I said. I took a deep breath. I knew the words I was about to say might be enough in themselves to send Nan riding off. But that wasn't the way I wanted us to part. "It's time for you to go on your way to Oregon," I said again. "I must ride with the braves because they will take me to their camp — where my father lives."

Nan's face looked puzzled. Then it took on a look of surprise. "Your father? Your father is one of the Sioux?"

"Yes. His name is Chief Running Bear. My name is Tall Dog among the Sioux. My mother was captured by them a long time ago. She lived with them for many years, and I was raised as the chief's son. When I was a young boy, my mother and I ran away from the Sioux. But now I am going back."

"To live with them?"

I had no answer to the question. "To see my father once again," I said.

I held out my hand to Nan. She just shook her head.

"I'd be dead if it wasn't for you, Johnny. I'm not going to run out on you yet. I saw the way those braves talked. You just might need my help yet."

I smiled at Nan's courage. "You just might be right," I said. "Pick up your rifle and put it away." We turned our horses and rode off to follow the braves into camp.

It was night when we reached the Sioux camp with the braves. Small fires lit the still bodies of the Sioux who stood to watch us riding in. Here and there, a soft glow of firelight shone from inside a tepee.

My heart began to pound as we made our way to the middle of the camp. It was like riding back into the past. I half expected to see a young Chief Running Bear at the opening of a tepee, his young, white wife beside him. But the chief was nowhere in sight. In the firelight, I saw only strange faces. Nan and I must have looked stranger still to them.

As we got down from our horses, several women came forward and led them away. Many braves gathered to look at us. But all were quiet.

In a moment, the brave who had spoken first to me called out to the others in a loud voice. *"I bring you a gift from the land where the sun rises. Look upon Tall Dog, son of Chief Running Bear!"*

No one moved or spoke. They just stood there looking at me — this stranger in white man's clothes.

I felt their eyes on me and reached to remove my hat to show my long Sioux-black hair. I let the hat fall to the ground.

"My heart is glad," I told them in their language. *"I have come home to my people."*

The brave called out again. *"I also bring you Tall Dog's white pup. I know you will give me no thanks for that."*

Now life came back to the Indians. All of them laughed.

Nan looked up at my smile and squinted. "Why in the blazes are they laughing? What did that brave say, Johnny?"

"He said he had brought two new braves to the camp."

There was no time to tell her more. As we spoke, another brave came toward us. Although the years had changed him from a child to a man, I knew at once who the brave must be.

"Why has Tall Dog left the world of the white man?" he asked. He spoke in English, not in the words of the Sioux.

"I am glad to see you again, Young Eagle," I said. "I have missed my brother."

Nan looked at Young Eagle and then at me. "He's your brother?"

"Running Bear had an Indian wife before my mother was captured," I explained. "She died young. Young Eagle was her son."

"You have not answered my question, brother," Young Eagle went on. He paid no attention to Nan.

"I have come to talk with Running Bear," I answered.

Young Eagle nodded. Then he looked at Nan and back at me. There was a second question in his eyes.

"She is a friend," I answered. "Her name is Nan Powers. We met on the trail."

Young Eagle's eyes grew dark when he spoke again. "You both bring the smell of the white people's world with you." Turning fast, he walked away.

I tried to forget Young Eagle's words. I turned to the brave standing next to me and asked him which tepee belonged to Running

Bear. The brave pointed to one close by. Telling Nan to wait for me, I walked over to the tepee and went inside.

Near the middle of the tepee, a small fire burned. Its logs were old and almost burned out. An old man with white hair sat behind the fire. He looked up as I entered, and the flames danced in his eyes.

"Come," he said from behind the fire. The wrinkles in his face looked even deeper in the soft yellow glow. He could see only my shadow against the opening of the tepee. *"Who is it?"* he asked.

"It is Tall Dog," I answered in a whisper. *"I have come to speak with my father."*

The old man's eyes narrowed. *"Come sit beside me,"* he said. *"These eyes of mine have grown old. They do not show me the world as clearly as they once did."*

I sat down beside the old man, and his eyes studied me slowly. In time his lips stretched into a smile, and he put his hand on my knee.

"I lost the boy Tall Dog," he said. *"But I am glad to see the man."*

I put my hand on his. The skin was tough but soft, like well-worn leather.

"I bring you news of my mother," I said to him. Then I told him several stories of her life in the land where the sun rises. As I spoke of her death, Running Bear stared quietly into the fire. I could tell he was seeing pictures there.

At last he looked up. *"She is not dead,"* he said. Then he put his hand on his chest just above his heart. *"She lives here."*

"And Tall Dog?" I said. *"I hope he lives there."*

"He has never left my heart. He never will."

Running Bear started to get up. But his legs failed him, and he leaned against my arm. He seemed to have grown lighter with age. He seemed smaller, too, as he looked up at me.

"You see a man who must soon sing his death song," Running Bear said.

"No," I said. *"I see a young brave who can teach others how to hunt and trap and fish. I see a young brave who can ride the wind and swim great rivers."*

Running Bear looked at me with tired eyes. *"So do I,"* he said.

* * *

That night there was much laughter in the Indian camp. Nan and I sat beside Running Bear and listened to the Indians sing old songs. I joined in some I remembered from my early years with the Sioux.

Our voices made a gentle but strong sound. They mixed with the other voices of the late summer night — those of the owl and the coyote. It felt good to be home.

A meal was prepared in my honour. I passed some of the meat to Nan. As she ate, I explained that the food was special. It had been cooked that night because I had come home to the Sioux.

"It's interesting stuff," Nan said. "What is it anyway?"

"Dog."

Nan swallowed hard. "Oh, no," she said.

5

Trouble in the Hills

Nan felt sick the next morning. The morning after that, we took a long walk beside the river. We talked and sat for a while watching the blue water flow on its way away from the Sioux camp. Then Nan looked at me. And she told me that she thought now it was time for her to move on.

She knew now that I was going to stay with the Sioux. And I felt that once she understood this, she would want to go. When we got back to camp, I helped her get ready. Then we rode together to a rise just outside the Sioux camp.

"Will you be heading on to Oregon?" I asked her.

"I think so. But I thought I'd drop back to see the Collinses first."

"Well, good luck."

We said a few more words and then goodbye. I watched Nan ride to the top of the distant hill. She turned to wave. Then she was gone.

* * *

Quickly I found myself fitting back into the life of the Sioux. Things came back to me that I thought I had forgotten. How to track an antelope. How to kill a buffalo with a single arrow. Soon I began to ride an Indian pony instead of my own horse. And I rode without a saddle. But I still wore my white man's clothes.

At times I caught Young Eagle watching me. I saw the look in his eyes. I wished that we could have been friends as we had been so many years before. But I knew that Young Eagle might never again accept me as one of the group. My angry brother would take his time. He would watch what I did and not listen to what I said.

I spent many hours with my father. Running Bear told me what life among the Sioux had been like while I had lived in the east. He was not happy with the way things had gone.

"The old ways are dying, my son," he said one day. *"Many of our young men are leaving the reservation. They go to live in the white people's world. Some of them work for the army and turn against their own people. It is a sad time for the Sioux."*

"But the killing between the whites and the Indians has stopped," I pointed out. *"That is a good thing, isn't it?"*

"It is. But it will begin again if braves like your brother, Young Eagle, have their way. Such Indians hate all white people. Many whites in turn hate them."

"Young Eagle has a reason for his feelings. He knows that some of the white people steal the Indians' land."

"Yes, the whites are trying to take the land from us." Running Bear nodded sadly. *"They do not love the Great Mother as we do. They cut down her trees to make room for their farms and ranches. They break open her body and take gold from it. They will kill our Great Mother in time."*

I watched the faraway look in my father's eyes as he spoke. When he finished, I was silent for a minute. Then I said, *"I read that the government now sends you money and food. Is that true?"*

Running Bear nodded, his face still sad. *"They treat us like babies who cannot care for themselves. Now our people look to the government to help them. They do not try to live as the Sioux once did. The old ways die."*

He fell silent for a time. Then he looked up at me. *"Tell me more about your time in the white people's world. Were you happy there?"*

At first I didn't know how to answer my father's question. There had been happy times. But there had been sad and angry times as well. I tried to explain.

"I went to school and learned many useful things. I can work with numbers. I can read books to learn what wise people have thought and done in the past. I can speak well to people, and some of them listen to me. But there are those who will not listen to a person whose blood is mixed. Such people call me half-

breed. To them I am not a person. I am only an animal to be hated."

Running Bear shook his head. *"It is not the blood that makes a person. It is the way you live that matters. There are Indians as well as white people who would kill a person to steal his blankets. No, it is not blood that matters, but the way you walk through this world."*

I said no more. I knew the old man's words were true. But it was also true that there were many people who did not believe such ideas. To them a person of mixed blood was worth nothing.

* * *

Life went on as days stretched into weeks. On one beautiful, clear day, I rode off into the Black Hills, I was riding towards a spot that was sacred to the Sioux. The sun was at my back. The heat felt good.

I stopped to watch a hawk as it flew in lazy circles across the sky. It came to a stop in the air, like a leaf caught on the wind. Then it dived to the earth. A minute later, it flew off, a small animal in its claws.

I turned to watch the hawk as it flew away. As I did, my eyes came to rest on a distant hill. I saw several riders on horses. They were coming my way. To my surprise, I soon saw that one of them was Ed Collins. As they came closer, Collins called hello. There were 13 men in all. Their horses were loaded with heavy packs. It looked as if they planned to hunt for gold.

I nodded hello. Then I asked Collins where they were going.

"Into the Black Hills!" he declared. "I just couldn't stay put another minute on the farm. All that gold's been calling for me to come and lay my hands on it."

One of the other men looked at me hard. He looked at my Indian pony and saw that I used no saddle. "Where did you get that pony?"

"Up north," I said.

"Have you seen much gold up there?" he asked.

"Not a bit."

"Hey! Why don't you join up with us?" Collins said. "There's more than enough gold in the hills for all of us."

"Thanks," I said. "But I'm not interested in gold."

Collins shook his big head. "That's right. Now I remember you said that back at the farm." Then he said to the men, "He's a crazy one!"

I studied the wild look in Collins's eyes and wondered at his words. Then I watched him and the others ride away. They were 13 crazy men making 13 tired horses run as fast as they could. The horses were kicking up dust and banging into each other. The men were shouting and laughing like happy children. Then they were too far away to hear. A minute later, they were too far away to see.

When I returned to camp, I knew at once that something was wrong. At first, I couldn't tell what. But then I knew. I ran to Running Bear's tepee.

"I didn't see Young Eagle in camp," I told him. *"Many of the braves are not here. Have they gone to hunt buffalo?"*

Running Bear's voice was low. *"They have not gone to hunt buffalo. They have gone to hunt whites."*

I waited for Running Bear to explain. Soon he went on. *"For a long time, Young Eagle has* wanted to make war on the miners in the Black Hills. I told him that would be wrong. We have promised the government that we will not make war. But now the miners have gone to look for gold near the sacred ground. Young Eagle says that they will destroy it."

"Yes. But I don't think that Young Eagle really cares about our sacred ground. He is just in love with war. He loves it, and he hates the whites."

Thoughts raced through my mind. It had taken me almost an hour to get back to the camp after I had watched the miners ride away. So it would take me another hour to return to that spot. Then it would take still more time to reach the miners' camp.

"When did Young Eagle and his braves ride out?" I asked Running Bear.

"Long before you came to my tepee. I could not stop them."

"I must go."

There was only one thing on my mind as I raced my pony over the dry, rough ground. I had to try to stop Young Eagle before he and the other braves reached the miners' camp.

My pony's hooves thundered over the ground. I saw no sign of Young Eagle and the other Sioux as I rode. But I was certain they had come that way.

The sun climbed to the top of the sky. Then it started to sink toward the west. I began to fear that I would be too late to stop the fighting at the camp.

At last I saw a thin curl of smoke rising into the sky. The miners' camp was just beyond the next hill. There was no sound of fighting.

As I reached the top of the hill and looked down, all seemed well. The Sioux war party was nowhere in sight. Dozens of miners were working quietly in the canyon. Some were panning for gold in the river. On a nearby hillside, I saw Ed Collins. I raised my hand to say hello.

That was when my fears came true. Before Collins could answer, a man near him screamed and fell to the ground. There was an arrow in the man's chest.

6

Attacked!

The braves exploded through an opening where the river cut through the rock wall at the west end of the canyon.

They came splashing down the river before the miners knew what was happening. Another arrow flew. Another miner near Ed Collins fell.

On the far side of the canyon, the miners there took cover behind a few big rocks. Some had their guns with them. They fired. An Indian fell from his pony and into the river. The pony kept going at a run.

But most of the Indians had rifles too. The miners who were caught panning for gold in the river had no chance at all. Young Eagle and the others killed them where they were.

Then a pony was shot out from under one of the Sioux braves. The brave never made it out of the water. Ed Collins found his gun and fired.

More and more miners fell. On the hillside right behind the camp, there were hardly any rocks for them to hide behind.

The Indian ponies followed the curve of the river south toward a second opening leading out of the canyon. The ponies without riders followed along.

Then suddenly Young Eagle turned on his pony. He seemed to be looking my way. And then I knew he would try to kill me. He could see me standing out against the sky. As I watched, Young Eagle took aim and fired. But his shot missed.

Collins returned Young Eagle's shot. But he missed also. Then the Sioux were gone as quickly as they had come. The river water still danced in tiny waves.

That was when Collins remembered me. He turned to look up at me on my pony on the rise above him. A bullet had grazed his large head, and there was blood on his face. He pointed his gun at me.

"It was you!" he cried. "You gave them the signal to attack!"

Then he fired. I felt pain shoot through my arm. The force of the bullet almost knocked me from my horse. I held on to its neck as it turned and started off at a run.

* * *

I reached camp before Young Eagle and the others. Running Bear saw that my wound was cared for. I told him what had happened.

I had just finished my story when Young Eagle and his braves returned to camp. They were shouting and laughing. Even though three of their men had been killed, they were happy with how things had gone — except for Young Eagle.

"Here is Tall Dog," he said loudly for all to hear. "Tall Dog was with the whites. What were you doing there, Tall Dog? Did you ride to warn them? Did you ride to fight with them against the Sioux?"

"I rode to stop you and the others. But I was too late."

"To stop us?" Young Eagle laughed. *"Better for you that you were too late. Or you would be dead now!"*

There was a wild look in his eyes. Then I saw them come to rest on the cloth wrapped around my arm. Young Eagle smiled. Then he looked at my face.

"No, brother," I said. *"The bullet was not yours."*

My words made him angry. *"You be careful, Tall Dog,"* he said, coming close to me. *"You had better live like a Sioux. Or you will die like a white!"*

Then he turned and walked away. Running Bear watched him go. His eyes were old and sad.

"It begins again," was all he said.

I put my hand on Running Bear's shoulder. There was silence for a moment as he and I looked at the ground. One drop of blood had fallen from my arm to mix with the dust.

All of a sudden, the silence was broken by a yell. A brave came running into camp. *"The whites from the mining camp!"* he called. *"They are coming here!"*

The Sioux camp moved quickly at Running Bear's orders. The braves got on their ponies. The women and children went to their tepees. Then Running Bear walked to his own tepee to wait out the trouble. Though he was chief, he was too old to fight with the braves.

As I took my gun from its holster, my feelings were mixed. I had grown up with the white people. I didn't want this fight. I'd never killed anyone, and I didn't want to. But I wasn't going to let anyone kill me. I took cover behind some trees.

Not far from camp, the miners were met by Sioux braves. The horses and ponies bumped into one another as their riders fought with arrows, bullets, knives and hands.

Soon the braves fell back to take cover in the trees. As the fight went on, both Indians and miners dropped to the ground. Some were wounded. Some were dead.

As the miners got closer to the camp, some of them rode off to one side and out of sight. I watched them go by and saw that one of them had a red bandanna tied around his head. It was Ed Collins.

I got up and ran around the tepees. When I

came to my father's tepee, I found Running Bear standing outside.

"Get inside!" I yelled to him. *"You'll be safer there!"*

But Running Bear didn't move. He didn't seem to hear me. There was so much shooting and shouting that I could hardly hear myself.

Then suddenly Running Bear spoke. *"My son!"* he cried out, looking past me.

I turned quickly and saw a man behind me in the trees. I pointed my gun at once. But before I could fire, the man sent a bullet screaming toward Running Bear's tepee. I fired. With a cry, the man fell into the bushes.

I turned around fast to help Running Bear. But he lay on the ground. The bullet had caught him in the chest. Running Bear was hardly breathing.

I picked him up and carried him inside. There I laid him on a blanket. He opened his eyes and looked up at me.

"The whites have brought me my death," he said. He spoke softly. His voice was little more than a whisper.

"I'll help you to live," I told him. I tore open the old man's shirt. There was blood everywhere. I wiped it away with my shirt. Then I could see where the bullet had entered his chest.

I took out my knife. *"I will take the bullet out of your body,"* I told him.

Running Bear shook his head. *"It is time for me to die. Put away your knife, son."*

Outside the noise of the battle grew louder. Then someone could be heard shouting orders. The shooting stopped, and it grew very quiet.

"Be still. I'll come right back," I told Running Bear. I covered him with a blanket. Then I went outside.

All the braves stood together on one side of the camp. The miners stood on the other side. In the middle of the camp were soldiers on horses. One of them, a man with long, yellow hair, stood in front.

"Who is the chief in this camp?" he asked. He formed his words slowly in the language of the Sioux.

"Running Bear is the chief," I answered. I spoke in English.

At my words, the man turned to face me. He stood like someone who was very proud of himself. He had a large moustache and blue eyes that were both quick and angry. "And just where might I find this Running Bear?" the man asked, speaking this time in English.

"He is in his tepee," I explained, pointing to the one behind me. "But he is badly hurt."

"I will speak to him," the soldier said. He pushed past me and went into the tepee first. I followed.

The soldier stood there with his arms crossed. He did not look at my father as he spoke. *"Chief Running Bear,"* he said loudly in broken words of Sioux. *"I am General George Armstrong Custer. Some of my soldiers saw what your braves did to the miners' camp. We followed them here to put an end to the fighting. Your treaty states that there will be no more fighting. You broke your word. By rights I should put all your people behind bars!"*

"A few of my braves broke the treaty," Running Bear answered softly. *"I am old. Some of my people no longer listen to me."* Running Bear's head rolled to face Custer and me. *"This is my son,"* he told Custer. *"His name is Tall Dog. Speak with him."*

Custer's eyes opened wide. *"This is a half-breed,"* he hissed.

"He is a man," Running Bear said.

"Sure," Custer said in English. His eyes narrowed meanly as he looked at me. "Now, Tall Dog, I didn't mean anything by what I said. You'll have to —"

As Custer was speaking, Young Eagle ran into the tepee. *"The soldiers want to take me to jail,"* he said. *"But I told them I must see my father and his son of the mixed blood who did not shoot fast enough to protect him. Perhaps my dear brother did not want to save the life of my father. Perhaps my father reminds him of the part of his blood he would like to forget!"*

"Silence!" It was Running Bear who spoke. *"You are a fool, Young Eagle,"* he said.

But Young Eagle wasn't listening. His eyes were fixed on me. "I will kill you, brother. I will kill you for letting my father be shot," he said.

Custer's eyes were on Young Eagle's belt. Several bloody scalps hung from it. "You'll kill no one else," Custer said angrily. "I'm placing you under arrest."

He reached out for my brother. But Young Eagle turned quickly and ran from the tepee. Custer followed him outside, running and yelling orders.

I heard the sound of horses as several soldiers rode out after Young Eagle. Custer was yelling for men to follow the other braves who had run off from the camp as well. His orders were to bring back every one of them — dead or alive.

Inside the tent, Running Bear listened too. *"I have lost one son,"* he said. *"But my other son has returned to me."*

Quickly he reached out and took my hand in his. Then he closed his eyes. In a very low voice, he began to sing his death song.

I sat beside him until the song ended and he was dead.

7

A New Chief

Outside Running Bear's tepee, several Sioux were waiting.

"Call the old men," I told a woman who stood nearby. *"Chief Running Bear is dead. Have them see to him at once."*

With a sad look, the woman went away. I stood without moving for a moment. Bits and pieces of my last minutes with Running Bear kept coming back to me. The touch of his hand. The Sioux words of his death song. His hand relaxing. The song ending.

I stood there letting the pictures come to my mind. I was afraid to stop them. I was afraid they would never again be so clear to me.

Then the angry voice of Young Eagle broke into my pictures. *I will kill you, brother. My* eyes shot open. Around me I saw the Sioux people waiting to see what I would do next. Some of Custer's soldiers still stood off to one side. The miners were trying to catch their horses so they could ride back to their camp.

Suddenly I remembered the man in the trees, the man who had shot my father. I made my way to the spot where he had fallen. A large man lay face down in the bushes. With my foot, I reached out and turned him over. It was Ed Collins!

I remembered that night in the Collinses barn. Nan and I had talked a long time. I had been dropping off to sleep when Nan told me what she had heard about Collins. Louise Collins had taken her aside and spoken openly about her husband's hunger for gold. Mrs. Collins had been worried that it would get him killed. And now, here in the Sioux camp, her worst fears had come true.

I passed my hand over Collins's eyes and closed the lids. Then I stood up. As I did, something on the ground nearby flashed in a beam of sunlight. Reaching down, I picked up the gold watch that Collins had been so proud of. I put it to my ear. It was still ticking. Slowly I slipped it into my pocket.

"Tall Dog!" Custer's voice rang out behind me. "Get your Indian hands off that white man. You touch a hair on his head, and I'll throw you behind bars before you can shout *hoka hey!*"

I stood up slowly and turned. I didn't like the icy look in Custer's blue eyes. I fought against an urge to rush at him and knock him to the ground. Custer's fingers were on the handle of a sword that hung at his side. *He wanted me to rush him.*

"I knew this man," I told Custer. "I shared supper with him at his house not long ago."

Custer sniffed but said nothing more. I walked over to where he stood. "What are you going to do to Young Eagle if you catch him?" I asked this man with the long, yellow hair.

Custer seemed angry at my question. "Try him in court," he snapped. "Then hang him!"

"Are you going to hang the miners too?"

Out of the corner of my eye, I saw the old men of the tribe come out of Running Bear's tepee. They stood watching and listening.

Custer's face showed surprise at my words.

"Of course we're not going to hang the miners," he said. "Why should we? They're the ones who were attacked!"

"The miners had no right to be in the Black Hills," I told him. "The Black Hills are part of the Sioux reservation."

"That's a government matter," Custer said. "I'm a soldier, Tall Dog. I was sent here to do a job. And I do it well."

Custer stood there, hands on hips, as if he owned the camp. He smiled as he spoke of his job. Then his smile faded. "You Indians are just making things worse for yourselves," he added.

"Why did the government send you here?" I asked him.

"To protect the miners."

"Then the government is breaking its own law. The government is protecting people it told not to come here."

"Your chiefs should have sold the land to the government when they were offered good money for it," Custer said. "Chief Spotted Tail and Chief Red Cloud should never have raised their prices at the last minute. They stopped the sale. If they had taken the money, there wouldn't be all this trouble."

Custer started to walk away, but I stepped in front of him.

"Young Eagle was wrong," I said. "He was wrong to make war on the miners. By doing so, he broke the law. But you also broke the law by coming here with your soldiers. I think you and the government are forgetting your own promises."

"Don't bother me with this talk," Custer said in an angry voice. "Tell your stories to the government, Tall Dog, not to me. I talk with *these*." Custer put his hands on his sword and gun.

He waited there for a second to see whether I would speak again. When I didn't, a small smile came over his face. He seemed to feel he had won another battle. He turned quickly and mounted his horse. Then he rode out of camp with his soldiers following. I watched the dust settle behind them.

When Custer and the soldiers were gone, the old men came over to me.

"Chief Running Bear is gone," one of them said to me. *"Now we must have a new chief. We have seen how you talked to the yellow-haired soldier. We want you to be our new chief, Tall Dog."*

The other men nodded.

"But I'm not —" My words stopped. I had been about to say that I was not a full-blooded Sioux. But then I knew that blood was not what mattered. What mattered was how a person walked through life. And what was in the heart. In my heart, there was a great love for the Sioux people.

For a moment I thought about what the old men were asking. Then I nodded and told them that I would be their new chief.

"But only if each of you will give me his help," I said to the old men. *"You have all lived long. You are wise. You can help me to be a good chief."*

Smiles broke out on the faces of the old men. They spoke to one another, and then they looked back at me.

"It is good," said the old man who had spoken before. *"We will kill a white dog and have a special meal to honour our new chief."*

"First I must go away," I told them. *"But soon I will return to eat with you and learn from you."*

In my pocket, I felt the heavy gold watch. I knew there was one more ride I had to make before becoming chief of the Sioux.

8

Trail's End

The morning sun was a soft yellow glow behind the clouds to my left. The autumn breeze cut through my coat with its coldness. I rode toward the south.

The sun was falling in the west when I found myself on a hill above the Collins' farm. The house and the barn looked small and lonely. The two buildings and the trees around them seemed hardly more than small bumps on the face of the earth.

I realised how little it would take to wipe away almost all traces of that tiny home except for the rocks from the prairie. A hard rain. A prairie fire. A band of angry Indians like Young Eagle.

People like the Collinses lead a hard life. They had to be tough, ready to stand up against whatever danger might come. As I made my way down the hillside, I found myself wondering about Mrs. Collins. She was a brave and strong woman. But what would she do now that Ed Collins was dead? Could she keep the farm running by herself?

Bang! The gunshot snapped me out of my thoughts. Bang! A second shot rang out. My hands went up into the air.

"Get down off that horse!" Mrs. Collins shouted from the window of the house. "And keep your hands in the air!"

"They *are* in the air!" I shouted back at her. "Don't shoot, Mrs. Collins! It's me, Johnny."

"Why, so it is!" She lowered the gun. "Come on in," she cried.

There was a smile on her face, but I knew it wouldn't stay there long.

"It's good to see you," she said at the door. "You must tell us all your news."

"Us?"

The door swung open, and I saw Nan sitting in a rocking chair by the fire.

"Johnny!" she said and ran to throw her arms around me. "Louise," she said to Mrs.

Collins, "When I heard you talking to some-body, I figured maybe it was Ed come home. Loaded down with gold!" She pushed me away so that she could get a better look. "But Johnny. I never figured ..." She smiled. "You're almost as good as gold."

I smiled back.

"Listen — sit." Mrs. Collins put a cup of cof-fee and a plate of food in front of me. I lifted the fork, but I didn't feel like eating.

"Have you left the Sioux?" Nan asked.

My eyes shot to Mrs. Collins. She just smiled back at me. "Nan tells me your father is a chief."

"I come only to visit," I told Nan. "Yes," I said to Mrs. Collins. "My father was a chief. He was killed two days ago — in a battle bet-ween the miners and the Indians."

The smile went from Mrs. Collins's face. "Ed has gone into the Black Hills to look for gold," she said. "Did you know that?"

I reached into my pocket and took out the gold watch. I put it on the table between us.

"Oh, no" was all she said. She picked up the watch and went quickly into the next room to be alone.

Nan reached out and put her hand on mine. "She'll be all right," Nan said, "It just takes time. She knew Ed might not make it back. We already decided I'd stay here at least until spring — until I had the baby."

She laughed at the look in my eyes. "That's right, Johnny," she said. "Charles's child. Maybe the child and I will live to see a better time."

"Johnny!" It was Mrs. Collins. "There are Indians on the hill!"

She came back into the room, and we all went to the front window together.

"Do you know them?" she asked.

It was Young Eagle and a war party of Sioux.

"Get the rifles," I answered. "We may have to fight."

"I'll use mine," Nan said. She and Mrs. Collins went to the front window.

I opened the door a crack and shouted through it. "Young Eagle, it's Tall Dog. I don't want to kill my brother. But if you and your braves don't ride away from here now, I will have to shoot."

At first there was silence. Then Young Eagle laughed.

"So we meet again, my brother," he called. "I should have guessed that I would find you hiding in a white man's house. It is where you belong. It is where you will die!"

Young Eagle gave a signal to his braves. They set fire to the tips of their arrows. Then they sent the arrows flying toward the house.

At the sight of the fire, I got off a shot from my Colt. It hit one of the braves in the shoulder. He held tightly to his pony's neck as he rode away. The fire arrows struck the stone wall of the house and landed on the dry grass.

"Mrs. Collins! Nan! Use your rifles!"

Mrs. Collins just looked at me. "But you said that Indian out there was your brother."

"My brother wants to kill us all. We must try to stop him. If that means my brother must die —"

I squeezed the trigger. My gun exploded to finish the sentence. The shot missed.

"The grass is on fire!" Nan yelled. "We'll be trapped in the house!"

It was true. The flames were spreading. "We'll have to go outside!" I shouted. "I'll go first. Then I can cover you. Stay in here as long as you can. Then come out shooting!"

If Mrs. Collins or Nan felt fear, their faces didn't show it. They nodded quietly and moved back to the window with their rifles.

I kicked open the door. I went through it as if I was being chased by wild horses. Firing fast, I hit a brave with my first shot.

Then a brave came at me from behind. His arrow bit into my leg. I turned quickly and fired. The brave slid from his pony and hit the ground hard. It was Young Eagle.

As I was staring down at Young Eagle, another brave came riding toward me fast. I turned, but there was no time to raise my gun. I saw the brave aim. But then a shot rang out from the house. Nan had fired. The brave let out a yell. His rifle dropped. He fell to the ground.

The pain from the arrow made it hard to stand. I dropped to my knees and shot at another brave who came riding past the barn. Then Nan and Mrs. Collins came out of the house. The three of us held our ground. And with Young Eagle among the dead, the other braves soon went riding up the hill and out of sight.

The fight was over. Nan and Mrs. Collins worked with buckets of river water to put out the fire. Then Nan came to me and cut the arrow out of my leg. She washed the wound and wrapped it with strips torn from one of Ed Collins's shirts.

The three of us sat by the river as the sun dropped from the sky and darkness began to set in. There was work to be done. But for now we just sat quietly. And I told Mrs. Collins the whole story of how her husband had died.

She shook her head. "It wasn't your fault," she said. "I'm sorry about your father and your brother. I'm sorry about this land and the way it turns people against one another."

* * *

The next day, we buried the dead. Then we fixed the damage done by the fire. We all knew the house would have burned to the ground if it had been built of logs.

In the evening, we rested around the fireplace. We talked about where our lives might lead us. We all agreed that, at least for now, we'd come to trail's end. Nan and Mrs. Collins would get ready for the long winter on that little farm just south of the Black Hills. And I would return the next day to my people — to become chief of the Sioux.